THE MYSTERY AT THE Space Needle

First Edition ©2016 Carole Marsh/Gallopade International/Peachtree City, GA
Ebook edition ©2016
All rights reserved.
Manufactured in Peachtree City, GA

Carole Marsh Mysteries™ and its skull colophon are the property of Carole Marsh and Gallopade International.

Published by Gallopade International/Carole Marsh Books. Printed in the United States of America.

Managing Editor: Janice Baker
Assistant Editor: Beverly Melasi-Haag
Cover Design: John Hanson
Content Design: Randolyn Friedlander

Gallopade International is introducing SAT words that kids need to know in each new book that we publish. The SAT words are bold in the story. Look for this special logo beside each word in the glossary. Happy Learning!

Gallopade is proud to be a member and supporter of these educational organizations and associations:

American Booksellers Association
American Library Association
International Reading Association
National Association for Gifted Children
The National School Supply and Equipment Association
The National Council for the Social Studies
Museum Store Association
Public Lands Alliance
Association of Booksellers for Children
Association for the Study of African American Life and History
National Alliance of Black School Educators

Once upon a time...

Papa said...

Why don't you set the stories in real locations?

That's a great idea! And if I do that, I might as well choose real kids as characters in the stories! But which kids would I pick?

MiMi, PICK ME, PICK ME!

ME, TOO, MiMi, PICK ME, TOO!

Christina

Grant

Pick me!

You two really are characters, that's all I've got to say!

Yes you are! And, of course I choose you! But what should I write about?

 National Parks!

SCARY PLACES!

FAMOUS PLACES!

FUN PLACES!

Disney World!

New York City!

Dracula's Castle

GRAND CANYON

On the *Mystery Girl* airplane ...

I can FLY Us anywHere!

Or aboard the *Mimi!*

Or by surfboard, rickshaw, motorbike, camel ...

Take me to the Forbidden City!

All great ideas! I can put a lot of history,

MYSTERY,

legend, lore, and laughs in the books! We can use other boys and girls in the books. It will be educational and fun!

Good stuff!

And can you put some cool stuff online? Like a Book Club and a Scavenger Hunt and a Map so we can track our adventures?

Of course!

And can cousins Avery and Ella and Evan and some of our friends be in the books?

Of course!

9

And so, Mimi, Papa, Christina, and Grant took off aboard the Mystery Girl and America's National Mystery Book Series—where the adventure is real and so are the characters!—was born.

START YOUR ADVENTURE TODAY!

1

WHAT'S A SPACE NEEDLE?

"Whooo-hooo!" Mimi shouted, as she raced into the kitchen.

Papa peered over the top of his newspaper. "What in tarnation has happened? What are you 'whooo-hoooing' about?"

Mimi fanned herself with the big envelope just delivered at the front door. "Oh nothing. Just the best thing ever has happened!" She pulled Papa out of his chair, and pumped his arm up and down as they danced around the kitchen.

Christina and Grant shuffled into the kitchen, still looking sleepy. Grant slouched in a chair at the table.

"OK, it looks like Mimi and Papa have finally lost it," Christina said, as she mechanically reached into the cupboard for their favorite cereals.

"What's up with them?" Grant asked, yawning.

Christina shrugged and weaved her way to the table around her twirling grandparents.

Papa spun Mimi around once more, then plopped down next to Christina. "I don't know why we were dancing, but it sure was fun!" He mopped his brow with his handkerchief. "I think I've had about all the excitement I can stand, without knowing what I'm excited about."

Mimi looked at Christina and Grant as if she hadn't noticed them until just then. "Oh, good, you're both up," she said. "Now I can tell everyone at the same time." She clapped her hands and shouted, "We're all going to the Space Needle!"

Grant and Christina looked at her curiously. The kids often traveled with their grandparents. Mimi was a children's mystery writer, and she often took the kids with her while she researched her books. But this time, they had no idea where they were going.

"What's a space needle?" Grant asked.

Mimi winked at Papa. "If you two don't know, you'll just have to guess."

"Is it a needle that goes into space?" Grant asked.

"Nope."

"It's a needle to sew something on a spaceship, right?" Christina said.

"Nope."

"Well, what is it then?" Grant asked impatiently.

"The Space Needle is in Seattle, Washington," Mimi explained. "It is a really high tower, and was built as a symbol for the 1962 World's Fair."

Grant listened while crunching his cereal. With his spoon halfway to his mouth, he asked, "What's a World's Fair?"

"Wait, what?" Mimi asked. She suddenly realized that the U.S. had not participated in a World's Fair since 1984. The kids had no idea what she was talking about.

"I'll be right back." Mimi quickly went into her office and returned with her tablet computer. When the little lights glowed to life, she leaned in toward Papa and the kids.

Mimi used her stylus to search, "World's Fair." She tapped on a site. "See? A World's Fair is when countries come together for an exhibition of industry, science, and technology. One of the goals is to present a spectacle people will remember. Here, I'll show you."

Mimi's sparkly red stylus flittered over the tablet. "The Eiffel Tower was constructed as the entranceway to the 1889 World's Fair in Paris. For the Chicago World's Fair in 1893, it was the Ferris wheel," she explained. She tapped on another picture. "Because of the world's fascination with the 'Space Age,' the 1962 World's Fair in Seattle centered on modern science and space exploration. They called it 'The World of Tomorrow,' and the Space Needle was built to represent it."

Papa pointed to the picture. "Back then," he added, "alien spaceships were presumed to look like a shiny moving disk, or 'flying-saucer.' And that's what they built the Space Needle to look like." He wiggled his eyebrows. "There were those who thought the Space Needle was constructed to send transmissions to other solar systems through its sky beam."

Mimi tapped her stylus on the glowing tower at the very top of the Space Needle.

"Whoa, would you look at that?" Grant shouted. "That is just soooo way cool!" He picked up the tablet and enlarged the picture with his fingers.

Christina tugged on his pajama top. "Hey, let me see too."

No response.

"Earth to Grant," Christina said. "Let the rest of us see it already!" She tried to snatch the tablet from Grant's hands, but he turned away.

"You're just jealous because I saw it first," Grant said.

"Am not!" Christina replied.

"Are too!" Grant continued.

"Stop!" Papa held up his hand, and gave them a stern look. He gently removed the tablet from Grant's grip. "You two cacklin' buzzards are wading into dangerous waters here," he warned. "This is Mimi's prized tablet."

Both kids sat back down respectfully.

"That's better," Papa said. "Now let's hear the rest of what Mimi has to say." He handed Mimi her tablet.

"Where was I, ah yes," Mimi continued. "Just think, if it hadn't been for the Space Age, we might not have put a man on the moon, or invented the Internet, cable TV, or cell phones!"

The kids gasped. "Well, I guess the Space Age was really important!" Christina said.

"And that ends my story about the World's Fair," Mimi said, closing her tablet cover. "So, we've been invited by my old college friend Connie Robertson to attend an event to raise money for needed repairs at the Space Needle." Mimi shook the envelope at Papa. "There are four airplane tickets inside this envelope!"

"Whooo-hooo!" Papa leaped out of his chair, and twirled Mimi in a circle. "Now this is what I call a great day! A dance with my honey—and FREE plane tickets!"

"There they go again!" Grant remarked, and giggled.

2

FINDERS KEEPERS

The family boarded the plane for Seattle. Grant was so excited he ran down the aisle ahead of the others. "Christina and I want to sit together," he called. He looked back. "Christina, I've got dibs on the window seat!" He turned back around, and smacked head first into an older man who was lifting his luggage into an overhead bin.

WHAM! The man's light gray hat with a small red feather flew off his head. An object popped out of his top pocket, and rolled unnoticed down the aisle under a seat.

Grant scooped the hat off the floor. "I am very sorry, sir," he said.

The man grabbed his hat from Grant. "That's my favorite fedora," he snapped.

"Watch where you're going, young man!" he added angrily.

Mimi touched the red beret on her head to make sure it was secure. She glanced at Papa, who knew she didn't want any problems with other passengers. Papa gave her a look of understanding, and caught up with Grant. "Hold on there, partner," he said. "You come sit with me, and Christina will sit behind us with Mimi."

Grant grudgingly took his seat. *At least it's next to the window*, he thought. After the plane was in the air for a while, Papa began snoring softly. Grant poked his head over the top of his seat to see Mimi behind him. "Hi!" he announced.

Mimi smiled at her grandson. His face and blonde curls were barely visible over the back of the seat. "Who's there?"

"It's me, Mimi!" Grant replied. "Whatcha doing?"

Mimi knew her grandson was bored and needed something fun to do. She held up her tablet. "I'm looking up Space Needle stuff. Want to see?"

"Sure," he said, and stuffed his face between the seats.

Mimi noticed Christina snoozing next to her. "OK, but we must speak quietly so we don't disturb anyone." Mimi pointed to her tablet. "See this? It's the SkyCity Restaurant at the top of the Space Needle."

Grant looked at the picture. "That's what's on top?" he asked. "It's just a normal-looking restaurant."

"Oh?" Mimi asked. "You were expecting Martians?"

"Well, ye-ah," he said with a giggle. "But seriously, Mimi, I thought it would at least have control panels and blinking lights inside. Papa said it looked just like something—what did he call it again?"

"A flying saucer," Papa mumbled.

Grant snapped his fingers. "Yeah, that's it," he said. "Well, outside it still looks like a flying saucer waiting to launch, doesn't it?" Grant pretended his hand was a flying saucer heading for outer space. "Whooooosssshhhh!!!"

"Grant, ssshhhh," Mimi said, then yawned. "I'm going to take a nap now." She handed her tablet to Grant. "Here, you can look at pictures of the Space Needle."

Grant took the tablet, and disappeared behind his seat. Once he got tired of the tablet, he toyed with his seat belt and played with his headphones. Suddenly, he spied an object wedged under the seat in front of him. He slid down in his seat, and used the toe of his shoe to scrape the object towards him. He picked it up and wiped the peanut crumbs off. It was an old Space Needle keychain, with a small rusted key on it. "Wow!" he whispered.

Just then, the flight attendant announced that the plane would be landing soon. "Yessssss!" he said. He was so happy to be landing in Seattle soon that he absent-mindedly slipped the keychain into his pocket.

As the plane neared the Seattle-Tacoma Airport, the flight attendant announced, "If you look outside now, you can see Seattle's famous Space Needle, built for the 1962 World's Fair."

Grant peered out the window and saw the Space Needle gleaming in the sun, with skyscrapers and snow-capped mountain peaks rising behind it. "Wow, Papa, look!" he called. The plane landed and taxied toward the gate, and the keychain was forgotten.

As the family piled into the hotel van, no one noticed the man in the light gray fedora with a small red feather frantically searching his pockets for his keychain.

3

SKY HIGH

Mimi was anxious to catch the monorail to the Space Needle where they were meeting her friend Connie for lunch. She wore a fitted red suit to match her red beret. She looked at her watch. "OK, let's get a move on!" she cried.

As they stepped onto the gleaming blue monorail, a man waved them in. "Hop on, everyone!" he announced. "I'm Joe, your operator." He pointed to the blue bench beside him. "You kids can sit right down here in front if you want."

Grant looked through the giant windshield and was thrilled at Joe's offer. "Wow! Really?" he exclaimed. He turned to Papa. "Can we sit next to Mr. Joe, Papa, can we?"

"Sure, partner," Papa said, ruffling Grant's hair. He and Mimi sat behind the kids.

"All aboard!" Joe yelled. With a quick blast of the horn, they pulled out of the station. "Welcome to Seattle, folks," he said. "It takes two minutes to get to the Seattle Center Station. We're 30 feet above any city traffic, so sit back and enjoy the ride."

Grant became more and more excited as they picked up speed. "Whoa, this is soooo wayyyyy cool, just like being on a roller coaster!" He raised his hands up above his head. "It's a-a-a little b-b-bumpy, though."

"I a-g-g-gree," Christina said, as skyscrapers and streets whizzed by.

As they pulled into the station and the monorail came to a stop, Joe pointed through the enormous windshield. "Walk down the ramp, and the Space Needle will be straight ahead." Joe smiled, and waved at Christina and Grant. "Don't forget to look up!" he said, pointing.

When the family reached the bottom of the ramp, the Space Needle burst into view, rising hundreds of feet into the sky. "Oh boy!" Grant shouted. "Let's race!"

"Wait for me!" Christina yelled. Her stick-straight, long brown hair flew out behind her as she ran.

"Whoa! Whoa! Whoa!" Papa called, but it was too late.

When Christina caught up to Grant, he was practically bent over backwards, trying to follow the elevator to the top with his eyes. "Can you believe how big the Space Needle is?" he asked. His blue eyes grew wide in amazement.

Christina craned her neck as she looked up, up, up, watching the elevator. She shaded her eyes, straining to see to the top. CRASH! "What was THAT?" she cried. She turned in time to see Grant tumble into a flowerbed along the sidewalk. His blond head peeked out of a sea of pink and white blooms.

"Grant!" Christina said. She grabbed her brother's arm and yanked him to his feet. "Are you all right?"

Grant brushed puffs of yellow pollen from his blue Spiderman T-shirt. "Yep," he replied. "I just wanted to get a better look at the top of the Space Needle. It's really up there!"

The family went through the glass double doors of the Space Needle pavilion and stepped into the crowded elevator. People crowded Grant from all sides, so he squirmed his way to the outside window. "I wanna be right up front!" he said.

The doors closed, and when the elevator slowly began to rise, the attendant spoke. "Good afternoon! My name is Jenna, and I'll be your elevator operator for the next, oh, 41 seconds," she said.

As the elevator climbed, Grant noticed that the people below resembled tiny ants moving quickly in different directions. They listened as Jenna explained how the Space Needle was constructed as an observation tower for the 1962 World's Fair. "The tower is 605 feet tall," she explained.

Grant felt his ears pop from the high altitude. Dizzy with fear, he glanced behind him and saw Mimi's hand. He took hold. "It's kind of scary up here, huh, Mimi?" he asked his grandmother. "Why don't I hold your hand so you won't be scared?"

Mimi smiled and took his hand. "Why, thank you, Grant, that's very sweet of you," she said. His secret was safe with her.

WHOOSH! The elevator doors opened, and Jenna announced, "We have arrived at the SkyCity Restaurant!"

As Mimi and Grant reached the doorway, a man pushed past them and dropped a folded piece of paper on the floor. He wore a gray fedora with a small red feather.

Grant grabbed the paper. "Hey mister," he called, "you dropped this!" But when he scanned the crowd, the man was gone. He unfolded the paper. It was a newspaper article about the evening event at the Space Needle. "Hey, that's where we're going tonight," Grant said.

Christina came off the elevator holding Papa's hand. "Wasn't that awesome?" She playfully poked Grant in the ribs. "What did you think, Grant?"

"I..." Grant hesitated.

"MIMI!" Suddenly, with a screeching squeal of delight, a tall woman with short brown hair ran up and gave Mimi a hug. "You're here!"

"Connie!" Mimi cried. Once she broke Connie's bear hug, she introduced Papa, Christina, and Grant to her dear friend.

Connie held Mimi's hands. "We have so much to catch up on!" She led them through the SkyCity Restaurant to a table where two children sat. "Christina and Grant, I'd like you to meet my grandchildren, Ethan and Ellie." Ethan had curly blond hair, and Ellie's long braids were dark brown. Both had sparkling brown eyes.

Once Connie was sure the children were comfortable, she led Mimi and Papa to the next table.

Christina tried to think of something to say to Ellie. She toyed with her water glass, and glanced out the window. She thought she was seeing things. The outside landscape was moving! Christina stood abruptly, and pointed. "Hey, those windows are moving!"

"No, Christina," Ellie said with a giggle, and pulled Christina back down in her seat. "Not the windows, only the floor under our table is moving. See?" Ellie pulled the snowy white tablecloth back enough for Christina to see the floor.

Christina blushed. "OK, I'm feeling really stupid right now," she said.

"Hey, don't worry," Ellie laughed. "This is a revolving restaurant. My first time here?" She rolled her eyes. "Ethan and I were with our grandmother. It was dark outside, so I didn't notice the floor was moving, and went to the restroom. When I returned, our table wasn't there, and my grandmother and brother were gone. I cried so hard, the manager had to go table-to-table to find them!" Both girls burst into laughter.

"What's with them?" Grant asked Ethan.

"Probably just girl stuff," Ethan said. "Hey, I made an elongated penny today. Want to see it?"

"Sure!" Grant replied.

Ethan pulled the coin from his pocket and set it into Grant's palm. A tiny Space Needle and monorail appeared on the front of it. "There's a machine right outside the Space Needle that makes them," Ethan explained. "You can keep that one. I have another one."

Grant was delighted with his new treasure. "Thanks!" he said.

After lunch, their waitress returned to their table. "Would anyone like dessert today?" she asked.

"Oh, you've GOT to try the Lunar Orbiter," Ellie suggested.

"That's a funny name," Grant said. "I'm in for that one!"

"Me, too," Ethan said.

"What is it?" Christina asked cautiously. She'd already had one embarrassing moment today with her little brother.

Ellie smiled. "Come on, it'll be fun," she urged. "The Lunar Orbiter is not a dessert, it's an adventure."

"OK, why not?" Christina agreed.

Within minutes, a parade of four waiters appeared. Each carried a glass goblet topped with a massive hot fudge sundae. A cloud of mist billowed out from under each goblet, like a rocket ship ready to launch. People stopped eating to watch as the waiters brought the dessert in for a vertical landing, mist hovering over the table.

"I love it!" Christina shouted, clapping with delight.

"This is the coolest thing ever!" Grant said. He shoved his spoon into his goblet, and lifted out a glob of ice cream and gooey warm fudge. After another bite, a ring of chocolate fudge formed around his mouth.

When they had all finished their desserts, Grant leaned back and grabbed his tummy. "Oooh, my tummy is so full!" he announced.

"What you need is some fresh air, little brother," Christina suggested. "Let's go ask if Mimi will take us up to the observation deck."

Mimi was admiring the view of Seattle through the large windows. "Connie, I'm so glad you invited us," she said. "This is so lovely!" She raised her water goblet in a toast, and the adults clinked glasses.

The kids approached the table. "Mimi, will you take us up to the observation deck with Ethan and Ellie, pleeeeease?" Grant pleaded.

Mimi smiled. "Sure, they can go with us as long as it's OK with their grandmother."

At Connie's nod, the kids raced to the elevator.

A chilly breeze swept across the observation deck. Mimi and Papa huddled together on one of the benches while the kids went sightseeing.

Grant zipped his hoodie, and looked over the side. "Hey, over here, you guys!" he shouted and pointed. "This is sooooo way cool!" The Space Needle had cast its shadow over the ground below, commanding the entire area.

"Wow, that is awesome!" Christina agreed.

Grant hopped up on a metal platform and scanned the horizon through the public binoculars. A majestic, massive mountain peak came into view. "Wow, look at this, Christina!" he called.

Christina took a look through the binoculars. "That's beautiful!" she shouted against the wind. "Look at all that snow on top!" She turned to Ellie. "How can that be? It's summertime!"

"That's Mount Rainier," Ellie explained, "and it's more than 14,000 feet high. It's really, really cold up there year round. Mount Rainier's peak is covered in glaciers, not snow." She paused and added, "And, it's an active volcano."

Grant snapped his head around to stare at Ellie. "A volcano?" he asked.

"It's true," Ellie said.

"When did it last erupt?" Christina asked nervously.

"It was a long time ago," Ellie said. "But it's an active volcano, which means it can erupt sometime. Scientists monitor it all the time."

Grant couldn't stop staring at Mount Rainier. Christina grabbed the hood of his jacket. "Let's go," she said. "We're going to the other side of the deck."

Jenna, the elevator operator, was leaning by the railing. She recognized Christina and Grant from the elevator ride. "Hi guys!" she said cheerily. "I hope you have fun while you're..."

RING! RING! Jenna looked down at her cell phone. "Oops, sorry, I need to take this call," she said. "Hello?" Jenna turned away from the kids, but with the wind blowing in their direction, they could hear her conversation. "Hey!" she exclaimed. "I think what you've been searching for all these years has been found. But it's being auctioned off tonight!" She hung up quickly and hurried toward the elevator. Christina noticed Jenna wipe tears from her eyes.

"Yoo-hoo, kids! Where are you?" It was Mimi's voice. "Hi, Mimi, over here!" Christina called. She stood on her tiptoes and waved to her grandmother.

Mimi tightened the red paisley scarf she was wearing over her hair. "Ethan and Ellie's grandmother just texted that it's time for them to get ready for the fundraiser."

"A fun racer?" Grant asked. "Mimi, can we go to that instead of that Space Needle event?"

Mimi laughed. "Grant, you *are* going. It's the 'fundraiser' I've been talking about, not a 'fun racer,' silly. It's the event to raise money to restore the Space Needle."

"Let's go, then!" Grant exclaimed. "We'll make some fun at this 'fundraiser' thing!" Christina grabbed her brother by the shoulders and giggled.

4

ORBITAL AUCTION

Christina gasped as they entered the Puget Sound banquet room. "Look how beautiful this place is!" she gushed. Crystal goblets and silverware glimmered under the chandeliers, while the twinkling lights of Seattle glowed through massive windows.

Connie wore a glittering, floor-length white dress. When she saw Mimi and her family, she cried, "Don't you all look dazzling!"

Mimi's royal blue chiffon gown shimmered as she moved, and Papa's black tuxedo and tall cowboy hat complemented her perfectly. Christina smiled broadly in her bright pink dress adorned with ruffles. Grant looked miserable in his light blue shirt and a striped tie. "I hate dressing up!" he mumbled through gritted teeth.

"Come, I'll show you to our table," Connie said. She weaved through the sea of round tables decorated with bright white tablecloths. "Oh, there's the mayor," she said to Mimi. "I'm sure he'll want to meet you. He's a big fan of yours."

The mayor shook hands with Papa and kissed Mimi's hand. "Connie, please make sure these lovely people attend my reception on Saturday evening."

"Will do, Mr. Mayor," Connie replied. She gave a quick salute and winked at Mimi. When they approached their table, Ethan and Ellie were already seated.

Christina's eyes lit on all the items waiting to be auctioned off as she sat next to Ellie. "Just look at all that stuff!" she exclaimed.

Grant turned sideways, trying to get a look at the items displayed nearest him. He didn't see any neat stuff. Most of it looked like a bunch of boring old junk to him. Grant tugged on Papa's arm. "When's it gonna start, Papa?" he whispered.

The lights dimmed and the room grew quiet. "Right now, partner," Papa said.

When the lights came up, Connie stood center stage. She spoke briefly about how proud she was to be a part of the Space Needle restoration. Thunderous applause rose from the audience.

A professional auctioneer joined her on stage. "Are you ready?" he shouted. The crowd cheered and clapped. "Let's open our hearts and our purses so the Space Needle can remain youthful-looking for generations to come!"

He smiled broadly. "And now, our first item up for bid is this lovely Space Needle water decanter and eight frosted glasses. Who wouldn't want this 'spacy' set in their home?"

People raised their hands to begin the bidding. Items came and went so quickly, Grant could hardly keep up with them.

"Now here's an item sure to be a hit in any galaxy!" the auctioneer announced. "It's a locked metal box that...let me see if I'm reading this right, was found in a hidden storeroom exposed during renovations to the Space Needle. We don't have the key, so its contents are a mystery, too."

Christina's eyes lit up, and she grabbed Mimi's arm. "Mimi, you should bid on that box," she whispered. "It looks really mysterious."

"Well, I..." Mimi began.

"Yeah, come on, Mimi!" Grant urged. "Just think, if there is a mystery inside, you can write about it!"

The auctioneer held up the box. "I'm starting the bid at twenty-five dollars. Twenty-five, twenty-five, twenty-five. Do I hear thirty?"

Mimi had worked up enough courage from the kids to bid, and stood. "I bid thirty dollars!" she shouted.

"Now thirty, thirty, thirty, do I hear forty?" the auctioneer continued.

"Forty dollars," came a man's deep voice from the back of the room.

"Fifty!" yelled Mimi.

"Sixty," the man's voice called again.

"Seventy!" Mimi hollered back. She couldn't see the man who was bidding against her. The auctioneer tried to entice others to participate. "Come on, folks," he said. "Don't let the bidding stay just between those two. Do I hear eighty? Eighty, eighty?"

"Eighty!" shouted a man standing near the windows.

"Go sit down!" someone in the room yelled, and everyone laughed.

"Ninety dollars!" the man in the back countered. He was getting angry. The bidding was heating up, and that silly woman had no clue what she was bidding on. But he did, and was prepared to go as high as it took to get that box.

"Oh dear," Mimi said, looking at the kids. "That's an awful lot of money."

"Come on, Mimi, don't quit now!" Grant cheered.

"Yeah, Mimi, buy that box!" Christina urged.

With an encouraging nod from Papa, Mimi raised her hand and said, "I bid one hundred dollars!"

Just as the man in the back was getting ready to raise the bid again, his cell phone rang. When he saw who it was, he picked up. "What?" he snapped. "Yes, yes, I'm bidding on it right now. No, there's some woman bidding on it too. I have to get back before..."

"SOLD!" the auctioneer shouted. "For one hundred dollars to the lady in the blue dress!"

The man snapped his phone shut and whirled to face the stage. Amid roaring cheers and applause, Mimi walked up to claim her prize.

"That's my girl!" Papa said. He escorted Mimi back down the steps, carrying the **oblong** metal box back to her chair.

"Yay!! I knew you could do it!" Grant jumped up and down, clapping wildly.

Christina and Ellie left the auction to go to the bathroom. As they entered the hallway, they heard a man with a deep, angry voice say, "Yeah...the box just sold. No, not to me, to that woman!" He kicked the wall. "I don't care what you're doing. Get on the next plane to Seattle!"

Christina yanked Ellie into the ladies' lounge off the hallway. "Did you hear what that man just said?" Christina asked.

"Yes," Ellie replied. She plopped down on the sofa, and fluffed out her green party dress around her. She seemed unaware of what Christina was excited about.

"Don't you see?" Christina asked. "I think that man was the other person bidding against Mimi. By the sound of that phone call, he really wanted that box!"

"Why?" Ellie asked.

Christina stood to leave. "Maybe once we open that box Mimi bought, we'll find out why!" she replied. As she stepped into the hallway, she spotted a scrap of paper outside the door. She picked it up and unfolded it.

THE BOX BELONGS TO ME!

Christina looked left and right, but there was no one around. "Come on, Ellie," she said. "I need to talk to Grant."

Neither girl saw the man in the light gray fedora with the small red feather standing in the shadows listening to them.

5

ALIEN APPETIZERS

When the girls returned to the table, Mimi's face was still rosy from the excitement of winning the box. It sat in the center of the table like a trophy.

Christina sat down next to her and toyed with the bottom of Mimi's earring. "So, Mimi, are you going to open the box tonight?" Christina asked hopefully.

"Oh, I really haven't thought about that yet," Mimi said. "But since we don't have a key, we'll probably have to take it somewhere to have it opened."

Christina was disappointed. She had to get Mimi to change her mind!

The savory smell of dinner wafted over from a long buffet table. Servers stood in front of steaming dishes to assist the guests.

When a server handed Grant an orange-colored soup as an appetizer, he nudged Christina. "This soup is orange," he whispered. "Who thinks that's just weird?"

"Just try it, Grant," Christina whispered back. "Listen, I need to talk to you about..."

Grant dipped the tip of his spoon into the soup, and dabbed it on his tongue. "Mmmmm, this tastes just like pumpkin!" he said.

The next server offered Grant a scoop of sliced potatoes. "Would you like some Yukon potatoes, sir?"

"Huh?" Grant looked shocked. He covered his plate with his hand and nudged Ethan. "Hey," he warned, "don't try the potatoes. The server said they were yucky potatoes."

"Not yucky potatoes, Grant," Ethan said, giggling. "They're YUKON potatoes! That's a certain type of potato that's really good!"

Christina pushed her food around on her

plate with a fork. She looked at Grant, who was eagerly devouring his meal four seats over. She needed to get his attention. First, she tried waving at him. He waved back and continued eating. Frustrated, she tried again. "Grant!" she called in as loud a whisper as she dared.

Grant looked up. Christina motioned for him to come over.

"What do you want?" Grant called out.

"I need to talk to you," she mouthed.

"What?" Grant asked.

Frustration won over logic. "I need to talk to you!" she shouted. People stared, and Mimi gave her a disapproving look.

Grant moved next to his sister. "Why didn't you just say so?" he asked.

"Grrrr..." said Christina.

"OK, what's so important?" he asked.

"Well, let's see," Christina said, and began counting on her fingers. "One, Mimi bid on a metal box that was found in a hidden storeroom. Oh, and it's locked. Two, someone else wanted it too, and kept bidding against her. Three, Ellie and I overheard a man on the phone telling someone he lost the bid. Four, he told that person to get on a plane for Seattle right away! And five, just look at this!" She handed Grant the note.

Grant read it and gasped. "Where did you get this?"

Christina explained that when they heard the man yelling, they slipped into the ladies' lounge to be safe. When they came out, the note was on the floor outside the door.

Ellie and Ethan sat wide-eyed while they listened to the brother-sister team analyze and speculate. "What are you two, mini private eyes?" Ellie asked.

A look passed between brother and sister. "Well, yes, sort of," Christina said.

Ellie drew in a sharp breath. "What?"

"My brother and I seem to get caught up in a mystery every time we travel with Mimi and Papa," Christina explained. "We're pretty good at figuring out clues and stuff."

"Yeah," Grant piped in. "This kind of stuff happens to us all the time."

"So, what do you think?" Ellie asked.

Christina smiled. "I think we need to get Mimi to open that box tonight!" She looked at the other three kids. "What we need is a plan on how to do that."

"Why would you need a plan?" Ellie asked. "Can't you just ask her to open the box?"

Christina sipped her water. "Because when I asked Mimi earlier, she said no," she replied. "Besides, we have to get up early tomorrow morning so there's no time then. We're going to Pike Place Market."

Grant looked at Ethan and Ellie, then snapped his fingers. "Hey, why don't you two come along?" he asked. "You can be part of our plan."

"Yes," Christina said. "We'll ask if you can spend the night."

"Sounds good," Ellie agreed. "That's a great place! And we know the area really well too."

Christina leaned in. "Here's my plan. When we get back to the hotel tonight, we'll drop hints about different objects Mimi can use to pick a lock."

"What kind of objects?" Grant asked. "I'm just a little kid. I don't know how to pick a lock."

Christina flittered her hand. "Oh, I don't know," she said. "We'll think of something."

"Count us in as long as our grandma says it's OK," Ellie said. "We have our clothes and stuff because we were going to spend the night with her anyway."

"Then it's agreed!" Christina declared.

As the family loaded into the limo, no one saw the man in the light gray fedora with the small red feather get into a taxi and follow them to their hotel.

6

A BLAST FROM THE PAST

Back in their hotel suite, Mimi set the metal box on the table. The sofa in the living room beckoned her. She took off her shoes, and Papa brought her fluffy red slippers. "Thank you, Papa." She looked around. "Where are the kids?"

"They went to their rooms without any fuss," Papa said.

"Uh-huh," Mimi said. She had a feeling they were up to something.

Just then, Grant and Ethan passed through the living room and waved. "Hi Mimi. Hi Papa," Grant said. "We just want a glass of water." As they walked past the table, Grant added, "That box really looks interesting. I bet

Mimi could open it with this safety pin if she wanted to."

"Or with this pen cap," Ethan offered. The boys set their items on the table and went back to their bedroom.

A few minutes later, Christina and Ellie appeared. "Hi, we want a glass of water, too," Christina remarked. They stopped at the table. "I bet Mimi could get that box open in a snap with this paperclip," Christina said, and laid it on the table.

"This hair clip would work, too," Ellie piped in. They scurried to the kitchen.

Mimi looked over the "tools" left by the kids. Papa picked up the bent paper clip. "They REALLY want you to open that box tonight," Papa said with a chuckle.

A few minutes passed, then the kids all ran back into the living room. "Mimi, will you pleeeeeaaaasssse open the box tonight?" Christina asked.

Even though Mimi was exhausted, she surrendered. "With all these great ideas, let's give it a try!" she said.

"YESSSSSS!" the kids shouted.

Everyone gathered around the dining room table. The air sizzled with anticipation.

"We'll try an old method first," Papa said, and held his hand out to Mimi. "Hairpin, please?"

Mimi pulled one from her fancy hairdo and handed it to him.

Papa inserted the hairpin into the lock and wiggled it back and forth. The lock didn't budge.

Mimi studied the lock. "I've seen a lot of keyholes in my time, but this one has a very odd shape," she observed.

"Oh my gosh!" Grant snapped his fingers and ran to his bedroom. He'd just remembered the Space Needle keychain he'd found on the plane. The key on it had an odd shape too. Grant tossed his clothing around looking for his pants. Finally, he saw them crumpled under the desk. He slipped his hand into the front pocket. There it was! He ran back to the dining room where Papa was now trying to open the lock with the paperclip. Grant tapped Papa on his arm. "Here, try this," he said, handing him the key.

Papa took the keychain from Grant. The end of the key looked like two "K's" facing each other. He slipped it into the lock, and it fit right in. "Well, I'll be," Papa said, scratching his head.

Mimi was puzzled. "Does the key work?"

"Seems it does," Papa said, and placed Mimi's hand on the key. "Please do us the honor." She turned the key. CLICK! The lock opened.

Everyone looked at Grant, then began speaking at once. "What is going on, here?" Papa demanded.

"Where did you get that key?" Mimi asked.

Tears welled up in Grant's eyes. Papa saw them. He sat in a chair and calmly pulled Grant onto his lap. "Now suppose you take it from the beginning, partner."

Grant explained how he'd found the key on the plane. "But when we landed, I forgot all about it. Honest Papa, I didn't remember until just now."

"I believe you," Papa said, ruffling Grant's hair.

"Well!" Mimi announced. Her mystery writer's mind was buzzing. "The key fit that lock perfectly, meaning someone traveled here on that plane to get that lock open." She stood over the box. "What do you suppose is so important in there?"

"Maybe there are diamonds inside!" Christina offered.

"Maybe there's a shrunken head inside," Grant added. When Mimi frowned, he smiled and shrugged. "Just sayin'..."

"Since we don't know what's in the box, you kids stand back and we'll open the box first. Then we'll let you kids see," Papa said. He turned the box to face him. "Here we go!"

Mimi clicked the button on the box and the lid sprung open.

The kids held their breath.

Papa's eyes grew wide. "Oh my gosh! Look what's inside!"

Christina screamed. "Ahhhhhhhhhh!!!!"

"Yikes!" Grant yelled, and hid under the table.

Papa bent over, and slapped his hands on his knees, laughing. "Just kidding!" he cried.

Mimi playfully swatted Papa's shoulder. "Oh, you!"

Grant stuck his head out from under the table. "Gee, Christina, you sure can scream!"

Christina fluffed her hair. "It's a learned skill," she replied.

The kids hovered over the table as Papa turned the box towards them. "These seem to be souvenirs from the 1962 World's Fair," he remarked. Papa carefully removed each item. "Five one-dollar tokens from the exhibits, three silver dollars, an old journal, a mold for a set of World's Fair tokens, and a photograph of three men," he said.

"Wow, look at all the neat stuff!" Grant shouted.

"Oooh, look at those shiny silver coins!" Christina started to reach for them, but Papa stopped her.

"Hold on, girlie!" he said. "Touching the bling will have to wait. Remember we have to get up early in the morning to go to Pike Place Market. It's late, so off to bed with all of you!"

"Awww, man!" Grant whined, and sat back in his chair with a huff.

Papa leaned over the table to return the items to the box and closed the lid.

Christina and Grant exchanged a look over his head.

Mimi and Papa turned out the lights and ushered the kids toward their rooms. "Goodnight all," Mimi said. "We'll see you in the morning."

But the kids had other plans.

7

A MYSTERY MEETING

The girls were reading when they heard scratching at the door.

Startled, Ellie put her book down. "What's that sound?" she asked, alarmed.

"Unless I miss my guess, it's Grant," Christina said. She opened the door, and the boys tumbled inside. "Why can't you just knock like everybody else?"

Her brother saluted. "Grant and Ethan reporting for duty."

Christina rolled her eyes. "You watch way too much TV," she said. "OK, here's the plan. I'll go get the box." She looked at Grant. "Don't make a sound, and do not leave this room!"

She stepped into the hallway. It was creepy in the quiet of the dark suite. Christina tiptoed silently past her grandparents' room. *What is that noise?* she thought. Heart pounding, she stopped to listen. Then, she recognized Papa's familiar snoring sound, and giggled. She felt a twinge of guilt as she lifted the box up off the table. She didn't mean to **undermine** Papa's authority, but she just couldn't wait another day to see what was in that box. She carried it carefully so nothing would rattle inside, and tiptoed back to her bedroom.

The kids gathered around the box as Christina opened the lid. She removed the journal, and set it on her bed. Then, she handed five copper-colored tokens to Grant. "Here, look for clues," she said.

Grant spread out the tokens on his bed. "Here's one of the monorail," he remarked, "and this one is for the Century 21 Expo." He picked up the next one. "Oh, this one's a really cool Space Needle one!" He flipped it over. "I wonder what this building is." He showed it to Ethan.

"Oh that's easy," Ethan said. "It's the roof of KeyArena. Well, it was the Coliseum during the World's Fair. We learned about it in school."

Grant picked up the last token. It showed the Space Needle again, but when he flipped it over, Grant noticed that the roof of the Coliseum was slightly different. He held both tokens up. On the first token, there was a line down the center of the roof. On the second, there was an extra vertical line running down the side of the roof.

"That's strange," Ethan commented.

Grant balanced one in each hand. "Hmmm, the one with the extra line feels heavier," he said. "Let's show Christina!"

Christina and Ellie were sitting on her bed examining the journal and the map. Christina pointed to some numbers. "There are several numbers here, and the words 'Space Cage.' What do you think that means?" she asked.

Ellie pointed to the numbers. "Those are longitude and latitude numbers. We studied them in school. But I don't know what a space cage is."

Christina flipped the page. "Oh, look at all these symbols and drawings," she said, pointing to the roof of a building.

Grant suddenly flopped down on her bed. Then he saw the building drawing and pointed. "Hey, that's the Coliseum roof, the same one on these tokens," he said. "That's what I wanted to tell you. There are two versions of the same token. And see? The drawing shows both views, and has a red arrow pointing to the roof with the extra line."

He held the tokens out to Christina. "Close your eyes."

She looked at him cautiously. "There better not be any spiders involved."

"No, seriously," Grant urged. "Close your eyes."

When she did, Grant put one token in each hand. "Notice anything different?" he asked.

Christina jiggled the tokens and motioned with her right hand. "This one's definitely heavier," she said. She had identified the token with the extra line in the roof.

"We should take these to a coin shop and see what they have to say," suggested Grant.

Christina handed him the tokens. "Good luck with that," she remarked, "since we'll be at Pike Place Market all day tomorrow, remember?"

Knock! Knock! "Christina?" Papa whispered, softly knocking on the door.

Christina sprang into action, and turned out the light on the nightstand. She pulled the blankets over her and Ellie. The boys did the same on the other bed. If Papa came in, they were so busted.

"Yes, Papa?" Christina hoped her voice sounded sleepy.

Papa cracked open the door. "I thought I heard you girls talking," he said. "We have to get up very early," he whispered. "You should be asleep like the boys."

"OK, Papa," she said.

The door closed. Christina waited five full minutes before she threw back the covers. "Whew, that was close," she whispered. "You boys get back to your room. I'll return the box."

"Sir, yes sir!" Grant replied with a salute.

Christina tiptoed down the hall, and set the box on the table, patting its top. "I'll keep your secrets," she whispered.

The Space Needle, shining brightly in the distance, held secrets of its own.

8

JUICY JOURNAL

"Good morning, kiddos!" Papa said, sipping his black coffee. "Did we all get a good night's sleep?" He winked at Christina.

The girls seemed to walk in slow motion. "Yes, sir," Christina said.

The boys plopped down at the table. "I'm too sleepy to know," Grant responded. He yawned loudly, and looked outside. "Hey, it's still dark!"

"We've got to get an early start to beat the traffic," Papa said. He pointed to the hearty breakfast delivered by the hotel restaurant. "Here, maybe this will perk you up," he said. Papa heaped three silver dollar pancakes on Grant's plate, slathered them with creamy melted butter and thick, warm syrup.

"Mmmmm, good!" Grant mumbled with his mouth full of gooey pancakes.

Mimi rushed to the table dressed in red jeans, a lacy white top, and sparkly red sunglasses. "I know I'm late," she gushed, "and I know we have to leave, but I just have to get my hands on that journal for a minute. Why, I could hardly sleep last night just thinking about it!" She lifted the lid of the metal box. "Come to Mimi," she said with outstretched hands. "I thought I'd start reading it with my coffee to get my mystery writing juices flowing."

Papa checked his watch. "Only if you can do it in ten minutes," he said.

"Point taken. So, maybe later then," Mimi replied, and slipped the journal back into the box.

A few minutes later, Papa escorted Mimi and the kids to the door. "Let's head 'em up, and move 'em out!" he called.

Grant stopped in the doorway. "Oh, wait! I forgot something!" He turned around and headed back inside the suite.

Papa was halfway down the hall. "Hurry up, Grant," he urged. "We'll hold the elevator for you."

Grant rushed back inside the hotel suite and lifted the lid of the metal box. He slipped the two odd tokens into his backpack. Then he rushed to catch up with the others. No one saw the man in a light gray fedora with a small red feather board the elevator next to them.

9

SOMETHING FISHY

The kids chatted in the van as they made their way to Pike Place Market. Even though it was still very early in the morning, downtown Seattle was bustling with people and traffic. Christina was amazed at the combination of old and new, as the 1960s monorail soared high above the traffic and zipped past towering skyscrapers.

The driver dropped them off at Pike Place Market. "Look how many people are already shopping here!" Mimi said. It was a happy, noisy place with hundreds of people shopping at various booths and buildings. As they wove their way through the crowd, Mimi opened the guide someone handed her. "According to this, the market is very historic," she remarked. "It dates all the way back to 1907 and covers acres and acres of land. Farmers and merchants do business here every day."

They stopped at one booth after another. At one of the berry farm booths, Mimi said, "Oooh, look, strawberry and raspberry jam. And oh, just look at that pepper jelly!"

Papa gestured the group towards a huge building. As they entered, the pungent odor of fish assaulted them.

"What stinks?" Grant asked, holding his nose.

"It's a fish market, Grant!" Mimi said.

Christina and Grant gazed at the huge salmon, enormous albacore tuna, gigantic king crab legs, and giant lobster tails displayed on tables among mounds of shaved ice.

Suddenly, a fish whizzed past Grant's head. "Hey! Watch it!" he shouted.

Ethan laughed. "Fish throwing is a tradition here," he said. "The man who threw the fish is called a fishmonger. See? People call out their order, and he tosses the fish to the cashier for them."

"Yeah, well, some traditions really stink!" Grant said, wiping fishy water from his face and hair. Christina and Ellie giggled.

Mimi hustled the kids outside. "Traditions are important, as you will soon see." She waved as she saw Papa approaching. "Papa got tickets for a walking food tour, but we must hurry."

Grant stepped up his pace. "I don't like to be late for any meal!" he stated.

They reached the pavilion just in time. "Hello, my name is Rose," said their guide, "and we'd like to share a taste of Seattle with you." She was a dainty girl with pale skin and a brilliant smile. "I think I truly have the best job ever!"

Grant's stomach rumbled right on cue, and everyone laughed.

As the group followed Rose, delicious, unfamiliar smells drifted out of several small booths along their tour route. "Now, we're not going to try everything today, because they'd need a truck to haul us back," Rose said. "But I think you'll like my choices."

The group sampled chunky clam chowder, ate succulent crab cakes, and munched on freshly made cheese. Papa dug into the Russian sauerkraut *pierogis* topped with sour cream, while Mimi and the kids sampled Italy's version of ice cream called *gelato*.

After filling their stomachs, the group headed back out into the sunshine. They could hear people clapping and cheering nearby, so the four kids ran ahead to see what was happening. They squirmed their way through the crowd to the front. Before them was a tall young man who played a guitar while balancing another guitar on his chin. And all the while, around his waist, he twirled two black and white hula-hoops, and danced.

"He's a street performer," Ellie said. "They play here for tips."

Christina clapped along with the music. "He's amazing!" she exclaimed.

"Look at him go!" Grant said, trying to imitate the dance steps. His feet got tangled, and he quickly lost his balance. "WHOOOAAA!" Grant shouted. He stumbled backwards as he launched over in a half-flip. His teeth clicked together as he landed atop something solid.

"Grant!" Christina shouted. She twirled around to see her little brother sitting backwards on a giant bronze pig!

The crowd laughed and applauded, as the kids helped Grant down from the pig's back. Someone handed him a dollar.

"They thought you were a street performer, too!" Ethan laughed.

"That's my brother, Mr. Showbiz!" Christina said. "Why is this huge pig standing right out on the pavement, anyway?"

"This is Rachel the Piggy Bank," Ellie explained. "She's the market's mascot. People feed her donations to raise money for good causes."

Grant slipped the dollar he was given into the slot on the pig's neck, and patted her on the head. "Enjoy your lunch, Rachel!"

"Come on, kids," Papa called from behind them. "There's more to see!"

As the kids turned to leave, Christina noticed a scrap of paper by her foot. She picked it up and unfolded it.

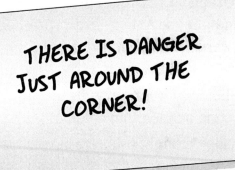

THERE IS DANGER JUST AROUND THE CORNER!

Christina looked right and left, but didn't see anyone looking her way. "Wait until I show the others!" she said, and raced after them.

10

TREASURE TOKEN

While Mimi and Papa strolled ahead of the kids to look at some hand-painted pottery, Grant tugged on the sleeve of his sister's hoodie. "I have something to tell you," he said sheepishly. "I brought the two tokens with me."

Christina stopped walking. "You did what?!" She searched her brother's face to see if he was joking. He wasn't. "You are so in trouble, little brother!" she scolded in her "big sister" voice.

Grant looked like he might cry. "I know I shouldn't have brought them," he whined, "but I thought maybe there'd be a coin shop here, and we could ask an expert about that one token."

Christina looked ahead at Mimi and Papa. "I haven't seen a coin shop, and what happens if you lose them?"

"I won't. I promise," Grant said, and crossed his heart. "They're in my backpack."

Suddenly, Mimi stopped walking and pointed at the window of an antique shop. "Oh, I simply must go inside and see that lamp!" she cried.

Christina looked where she pointed and couldn't believe their luck. A shop named The Coin Exchange was right next door to the antique shop! "Mimi, can we go into that coin shop over there and look around while you shop?" Christina asked quickly.

"I'll go with them," Papa said, "while you look at your lamp."

Papa and the kids entered the coin shop. Papa immediately struck up a conversation with an older man looking at some World War II memorabilia near the entrance.

A bell chimed, and a man came out of the back room. "Ah, good morning, children. My name is Tom."

A security guard standing near the door suspiciously watched their every move. His eyes reminded her of a hawk, ready to pounce.

Christina looked back at Papa to make sure he was occupied. "My brother has a couple of tokens we'd like you to examine," she said.

Tom looked surprised. "Tokens? This is a coin shop, not a token shop."

Grant stepped up to the counter. "But they're from the 1962 World's Fair," he argued. "And one of them seems to be very unusual." Grant explained about the Coliseum roof having an added line, and the extra weight of the coin.

"Please, Mr. Tom?" the kids pleaded.

Tom looked at their hopeful faces, and sighed. "Ah, the World's Fair. All right, let me have a look at them." He held both tokens in his hand and could feel the weight difference. But he noticed something else about the heavier token. "This feels sort of rubbery," he said. "Here, let me try something." He placed the token on his worktable and held up a small bladed tool. "May I?"

Grant nodded his head.

Tom carefully scraped at the finish around the edge, and a flash of silver showed through. Tom looked up. "Why, this is no token," he exclaimed. "Unless I'm mistaken, there's a silver dollar under here!"

"What?" Grant said. He looked at Christina.

The guard suddenly seemed very interested in what they were saying. He leaned on the counter, and narrowed his eyes at Grant. "Where'd you get that, son?"

Just then, Papa called to the kids. "Mimi is ready to go, kiddos," he said. "Let's get a move on." Christina was relieved. She didn't like the way Hawk Eyes was leering at Grant. "Gotta go!" she said.

Tom handed Grant the tokens and Christina practically pushed the kids out the door.

The guard rubbed his chin. "Those sure were interesting tokens, weren't they, Tom?" Before he could answer, the bell on the door chimed and another customer came in.

No one saw the security guard dash into the back room and make a phone call.

11

SILVER DOLLAR SWINDLE

The minute they stepped outside, Grant danced around, wiggling from head to toe. "Yes!" he shouted. "Did you hear that? We just discovered a mysterious clue about one of the Space Needle tokens!"

"Be quiet, Grant!" Christina warned, looking back at the shop. "That guard in there gave me the creeps and I don't want to draw his attention."

Questions swirled through her head about the mystery that was unfolding before them. *What did silver dollars have to do with the World's Fair? Why was a silver dollar disguised to look like a token?* She had a feeling that they could be mixed up in something they shouldn't be mixed up in! She needed to do some research to find some answers.

While Mimi and Papa wandered in and out of more booths, Christina and Ellie used Mimi's cell phone to research silver dollars at the 1962 Seattle World's Fair.

"Look," Christina said. "It says here that one of the premier attractions at the World's Fair was a million-dollar display of silver dollars." She pointed to a photograph of the two giant semi-trailer trucks that carried the silver dollars cross-country to Seattle for the World's Fair. "The article says that there was an opportunity for fair-goers to pose with the silver dollars and have their pictures taken. They would buy the photograph, and after the fair ended, a silver dollar from the display was supposed to be mailed to them.

"But check this out," Christina added, pointing to the "Comments" section below the article. "Look how many people over the years said they never received their silver dollar."

"What do you think it all means?" Ellie asked.

"**Offhand**, I don't have a clue." Christina said. Suddenly, she looked up and snapped her fingers. "Clue! I nearly forgot," she added. "I found this scrap of paper on the pavement right after we rescued Grant from the pig." She removed it from her pocket to show it to them. "Come see, Grant." She turned all the way around in a circle. "Where's Grant?"

"He was standing right here a minute ago," Ethan replied.

The kids stood at the corner of two streets. Christina looked up one street and down the other. Grant was nowhere in sight. She had no idea which way to go and began to panic. "What are we going to do? What if we can't find Grant?" she cried.

"Don't worry," Ellie said. "We grew up around here. We'll find Grant."

Ethan headed to a nearby bus stop. He scouted the bench and ran back waving a folded piece of paper in the air. "Here!" he said. "I found this tour booklet. Maybe it will give us some ideas." Inside was a map of the market and photos of buildings in the surrounding area.

As Christina scanned the booklet, one building in particular caught her eye. She tapped on the picture. "This building looks familiar. Do you know what this is?" she asked.

Ethan glanced at the photo. "Sure," he replied, "it's KeyArena. It used to be..." He started running. "Come on, you guys!" he yelled. "I know where Grant is!"

12

BUBBLEATOR BLASTOFF!

As the kids raced to the arena, Christina spotted a blond head bobbing up and down near the massive entryway. "That's...got...to be...Grant!" she shouted, breathing hard from sprinting.

Christina grabbed Grant's bony shoulders. "Just...what do you think...you're doing?" she asked.

"I just had to see it, Christina," Grant said, almost reverently. "Can we go inside, please?" he asked. Fascination won out over logic. Christina pushed open the glass doors and the kids stepped inside the arena. "Can you believe how huge this place is?" she asked. Her voice echoed.

The boys stared at enormous pictures of Seattle basketball players in motion and famous rock star posters plastering the walls. But Christina discovered a separate area where a whole wall was dedicated to photos and memorabilia of the 1962 World's Fair and the Century 21 Coliseum.

Grant and Ethan burst into the room behind the girls. "Wow, look at these old pictures from the World's Fair!" Grant said.

As Christina stepped along the roped-off walkway, she saw gleaming photos of the Space Needle lit up at night and a photo of something called the "Bubbleator." Christina read the plaque next to it that described the history of the huge, sphere-like glass elevator that had been nestled in the center of the Coliseum. Basked in its golden light, about 100 people at a time were transported to and from the World of Tomorrow exhibit.

"Oh look," Christina clapped her hands. "There's a picture of the million-dollar display!" The photo showed the gigantic wire corn crib where the money had been kept, with several security guards guarding the display. Suddenly, Christina paused. "Are you kidding me?" she asked in amazement.

"What is it?" Grant said, running over next to her.

She touched her fingertip to the photo. "See that guy right there?" she asked. "I think he's that creepy Hawk Eyes, the security guard from the coin shop! He was a lot younger in this photo, but I'd recognize those steely eyes anywhere," she said with a shudder.

Christina's sightseeing mood was spoiled now. "Come on, let's get back to the market before we're missed," she warned. She started to herd the kids towards the door when she noticed a scrap of paper sticking out of the frame of the picture. She plucked it from the frame and opened it.

THEY KNOW YOU HAVE THE TOKENS!

Christina scanned the area, but saw no one. Her mind began racing. Who was giving her these clues? Why was she getting them? Why didn't the person just come up to them, and tell them what they wanted? Did they need to remain anonymous for some reason? Why???

13

SKY HIGH

When the kids returned, Mimi and Papa were just coming out of a shop.

"Yooo-hooo, kids!" Mimi waved. "Here we are!"

Weighed down with shopping bags, Papa grinned at the kids. "I hope you all have some energy left," he said, "because we're heading to the Waterfront!"

A van dropped the group off at Pier 57, where they got their first look at the Seattle Great Wheel.

"That's the biggest, most giantist Ferris wheel I've ever seen!" Grant shouted.

"Is 'giantist' even a word?" Christina teased, arm in arm with Ellie.

Grant frowned at this sister and grabbed his grandmother's hand. "Seriously, Mimi, how tall do you think it is?" he asked.

"I've read that the Seattle Great Wheel is 175 feet tall," Mimi replied.

At Mimi's comment, the kids stopped and looked up. From where they stood, the top of the gleaming metal wheel seemed to disappear into the puffy white clouds.

Papa rushed to purchase tickets and they hurried to get in line. But the line to ride the wheel was wrapped around the line-lanes twice. While Papa stood in line, Mimi and the kids wandered over to a nearby building. "Come on, kids," Mimi said. "Here's something to do while we're waiting—let's take some fun photos!"

Inside, a photographer offered the kids a variety of silly backgrounds for their photos. The kids chose one of them as puppies riding the Seattle Great Wheel.

"Look at me! I'm a little Chihuahua," Christina said. "Arf! Arf!" she barked, then burst out laughing. "This is so much fun!" Ellie said, giggling.

Soon they were all acting silly, barking like dogs. Grant and Ethan got down on all fours, and howled a popular song. The photographer explained they could pick up their photos after the ride.

As they exited the building, Papa was waving his arms frantically for them to hurry. They raced toward him and scrambled onto the spacious, all-glass gondola. SNAP! The doors closed firmly.

Grant suddenly remembered his ride on the Space Needle elevator. "Ah, maybe I should stay on the ground here with Mimi so she doesn't get scared," he said nervously.

"Don't worry, Grant," Mimi whispered. "I'll be right here with you."

Slowly, slowly, slowly the car rose. Soon, a panoramic view of the Seattle skyscrapers burst into view. Christina especially enjoyed gazing through the top of the glass car as they climbed. "We must have the best view in the whole city!" she exclaimed.

Grant's blue eyes darted up, over, and sideways, looking out through the large glass windows at the colossal wheel. He was trying hard not to be terrified, but he was also curious about the workings of the giant machine. "Hey, Mimi," he asked, "why is this called a Ferris wheel? What's a ferris?"

Mimi smiled. "Ferris isn't a what, Grant, it's a who," she explained. "The Ferris wheel was named after George Washington Gale Ferris, Jr., who created it for the 1893 World's Fair."

"Whoa, that's awesome!" Grant said, amazed that someone could have a carnival ride named after him.

Everyone in the car got eerily quiet after that, absorbed in the view as they climbed higher and higher, until they reached the very top. "Hold on tight," Ethan told Grant. "Here comes the best part!" The wheel jerked to a stop, and the car swayed back and forth a little, giving them a feeling of floating on the blue waters of Puget Sound, over 100 feet below. Then with a bump and a thump, the wheel started to move again.

The kids giggled with glee. Looking outside, Mimi couldn't imagine a better backdrop for pictures. "One, two, three... selfie!" Mimi said, as she snapped a picture of the whole gang.

When they had completed one full turn around the wheel, Grant thought, *Whew, we're done. That wasn't so bad.* But with a click-ka-ty-clack, the gondola brushed over the exit platform and began to climb again.

14

BACKPACK SWITCHEROO

When the group climbed out of the gondola, it wasn't Grant, but Papa who was holding his stomach. His face was pale. "I'm kind of queasy from the ride," he sputtered. "I think three times around was a little much, don't you?"

"Yes, dear," Mimi said calmly, as she led him to a picnic table under a shady tree.

Grant said, "But Papa, we have to pick up our photos."

"I think I need to sit this one out, little partner," Papa mumbled.

Mimi stepped in to help. "Christina, the building is right over there," she pointed. "Will you please take Grant and go pick up the photos?" As they walked away, Mimi called, "And come right back here."

Christina was puzzled about getting another clue and needed to discuss it with her brother. "Someone's been following us," Christina blurted out.

Grant stopped. "There's been someone following us? When? Where?" Grant turned in a circle. "I haven't noticed anyone. Besides, what would someone want from us?"

Christina showed him the note she received at the market, and the one from the arena. "Apparently, it has something to do with those tokens in your backpack." She rubbed her arms as if chilled. "I can't figure this out, or who is leaving these clues."

Grant surprised his sister by opening the door for her. "It'll be OK, Christina," he whispered. "We've been through stuff like this before, and don't we always end up solving the mystery?" he asked with a wink.

As they entered, an elderly security guard with a bushy white mustache was holding a photo while talking on his phone. He hung up when the bell sounded and handed the photo to the cashier. The kids didn't see that the photo the guard had been holding was of them.

The cashier carefully wrapped their packet of photos. "Be careful not to bend them," he warned. Christina started to put the photos in her backpack, but noticed that Grant's had more room. "Let's put them in yours," she suggested.

"OK." Grant poked his head up over the counter and hefted his backpack on top. He started shifting items from his backpack to hers starting with a flashlight, spy glasses, and glue sticks. Lastly, he pulled out the two tokens.

Christina noticed the security guard's eyes light up when he saw the tokens. *What does THAT mean?* she thought.

Hurry, Grant, she silently pleaded. *Why is the guard so fixated on the tokens? Will he try to grab them?* She sighed with relief when Grant finally slipped the tokens into her backpack. She shoved the photos into his backpack and ushered him out the door. In her haste to escape the security guard, Christina did not realize they had exited out the opposite door from where they had come in. They were heading into a dead end, and the security guard smiled as he followed them outside.

15

A CHILLING CHASE

Soon, Grant heard footsteps pounding on the pavement behind him. He whirled around to see the security guard heading toward the kids. "Christina, that security guard is following us!" he cried.

Christina glanced back. "I was afraid of that," she said. "When he saw us do that backpack switcheroo, his eyes lit up when he saw those tokens!"

"So?" Grant asked, confused. He skip-walked to keep up with Christina.

The security guard walked faster now too.

"It means he's after the tokens, Grant!" she yelled. "Let's get out of here, fast!" They broke into a run.

The guard stumbled as he began to chase them. He got closer with every stride!

Christina led Grant to where she thought they'd left Mimi and Papa. But they were gone!

"Where's Mimi and Papa!?" puffed Christina. She scanned the benches and trees as they zig-zagged through a grassy area. Once they saw the security guard gaining on then, they sliced through crowds trying to lose him.

Christina saw a ladies' bathroom and quickly grabbed Grant's arm. They ducked inside. "I think...we're safe...now," she said, trying to catch her breath.

Grant looked around and saw a woman putting on lipstick in front of a mirror. "Uh, Christina," Grant whispered. "We're in the girls' bathroom!"

"So?" Christina snapped. Heart pounding, she listened for footsteps following them inside the bathroom, but heard nothing.

Grant flapped his arms like a bird. "So, I'm a boy! Don't you think anyone will notice?" he shouted.

"Shhh! I hear you, Grant!" Christina said. She snuck under a windowsill and peeked over the ledge. The guard stood outside the building with his back to them. He leaned against a light post, panting. She looked at Grant and motioned her head toward the window. "Everyone can hear you!"

When Grant saw the security guard, his eyes got wide and he flattened himself against a wall. "Do you really think he heard me?" he asked. His eyes locked on Christina's. "Do you think he'll come in here after us?"

Christina didn't stop to answer. She took Grant by the hand and scrambled out the back door. They continued running to the other side of the photo building, where she saw Mimi, Papa, Ethan, and Ellie calmly sitting on a shady picnic table.

What she didn't see was the guard yank out his phone and make a call.

16

SNAKES AND SPICES

Christina looked around and breathed a sigh of relief that the security guard hadn't followed them. She and Grant arrived at the picnic table looking a little **disheveled**, but happy to be safe with their family and friends.

Mimi saw her grandchildren's flushed faces and windblown hair, and suspected there was a story to tell. "So how did it go picking up the pictures?" she asked.

"Fine!" both kids said quickly.

"Uh-huh," Mimi said, not convinced at all.

Trying to distract her, Grant groaned and rubbed his tummy. "Please, Mimi, I need something to eat," he begged. "Pleeaasssee!"

Mimi let it go—for now. "Well, seeing that Papa's world is upright again, let's head over to the Chinatown-International District," she suggested.

"Yesssss!" Ethan and Grant said with a high-five.

The sights, sounds, and smells of Chinatown amazed the kids. Food vendors dishing up a variety of hot, juicy meats and spicy sauces packed the already crowded streets.

"Oooh, look at that!" Grant said each time they passed another food booth.

Mimi chose a cozy table on an outdoor patio. At a booth nearby, a tiny woman in an orange apron stirred a steaming pot. Mimi asked her, "Excuse me, it seems quite crowded and loud here. Is something special going on?"

The lady smiled broadly. "It is Dragon Fest," she replied. "You and your family should stay for the parade later." Mimi nodded. "Thank you!" she said.

Papa bought tickets for a food sampling. Each person had a plate with six shallow spots for their food choices. Ellie was the first to fill her plate. She came back with an extra dish piled with small cubes of fried meat that smelled spicy.

Christina sniffed the dish. "Mmmm, that smells really great!" she said.

Ellie put a few cubes of the meat on Christina's plate, and then on Grant's. "Here, try some," she urged with a smile. "It's just delicious!"

Christina stabbed her fork into a piece of the meat and blew softly on it to cool it. "What is it?" she asked.

Ellie grinned. "Fried snake meat," she replied.

Christina studied her dish, made a face, and shook her head. "Sorry, I don't think I can eat this," she mumbled.

Grant's eyes got wide. "Snake meat! There's no way I'm eating that!" He pushed his plate away. "Snakes belong on the ground, not in my tummy!" He stubbornly folded his arms over his chest.

"Just try a tiny bite," Ellie coaxed, "and if you hate it, don't eat it." She handed Christina a set of chopsticks.

"Ok, here goes," said Christina. She had some trouble holding the chopsticks, but finally got the hang of it and was able to lift a tiny piece of meat. She held her nose, closed her eyes, and popped it into her mouth. She chewed cautiously at first, and was surprised at how good it tasted. "Wow!" she exclaimed. "This tastes really good!"

"Try yours," Christina urged Grant. "Here, open your mouth and I'll pop it right in." She held up a small piece of snake meat in her chopsticks for Grant.

Grant looked sideways at his sister. "OK, but no funny stuff!" He squeezed his eyes shut and stuck out his tongue. As soon as he felt the meat land on it, he started chewing quickly. "Mmmm, it's kinda' chewy." He closed one eye as he made his decision. "But I like it!"

The kids laughed. "Now you can go back home and tell your friends you ate fried snake!" Ethan said.

Mimi and Papa had finished dinner and stood. "We're going to go check out the desserts and bring back something yummy," Mimi promised.

As soon as they left the table, the kids huddled together. Christina took the scraps of paper out of her backpack and spread them on the table. "So, let's figure out where we are with this mystery," she said. "Mimi bought a mysterious locked box at the auction. Then, Ellie and I overheard a man on the phone tell someone he lost the bid. He told that person to get on a plane for Seattle right away! Then Grant ended up having the key to open the box. Later he discovered that a token in the box felt different from the others, so we took it to a coin shop and discovered it was really a silver dollar. And these notes!" Christina picked up one of the notes and shook it. "I think these are warnings from someone!"

"But why would someone do that?" Ellie asked.

"Because we may have gotten ourselves involved in something dangerous when Mimi won that box," Christina replied. She gave the kids a serious look. "I hope we can find out what it is before it's too late!"

17

DRAGON SURPRISE

Mimi and Papa returned carrying shiny fruit perched on a long stick. "Look what I have here!" Mimi announced, handing a stick to each of them. "This is called *bingtanghulu*." The kids stared at the tower of strawberries, pineapples, and crabapples that had been dunked in thick, sugary syrup and hardened into rock candy. They shined like jewels!

"Gimmie, gimmie," Grant said with outstretched hands. But before he could sample the sweet treat, a loud BANG pierced the air. Grant jumped out of his seat at the sudden noise. "What's THAT?" he asked.

"It's fireworks!" Ellie replied, clapping. "The Dragon Fest parade is starting!"

Just then, a band of drummers in bright red and gold uniforms marched up the street. People cheered and waved mini-dragons on sticks.

"What's up with all the dragons?" Grant asked.

"In China, dragons are considered magical and ward off evil spirits," Ethan said. "The festival is to honor them."

The parade soon became even more colorful and exciting as street dancers in hot pink, orange, gold, and turquoise costumes stepped to the rhythm of the drums.

The kids danced and laughed while the music played. "Watch me!" Grant shouted as he tried to **mimic** the dance steps. When he added a little extra spin move, his feet tangled and he started to fall. "Ahhhhh!" Grant shouted as he tumbled into a pile of rags sitting by the curb. A tattered gray rag toppled onto his head. "Poof! Poof!" Grant puffed, trying to blow it away from his face so he could see.

Ethan tried to hide a giggle. "Hey, dude! Are you OK?" he asked.

"Yes," Grant grumbled, embarrassed. He bent over to shake the rags off his shoes. When he stood up, he was startled to see an enormous, snake-like dragon coming right at him! He could see people's feet beneath the dragon, steering the colorful creature as it zig-zagged through the street.

Just as the dragon got close, it shifted directions. As its tail started to pass by, the tail lifted up and the boys found themselves face to face with the security guard from the coin shop.

"Give me those tokens, now!" he demanded.

He came so close they heard his demand clearly, even over the banging of the drums and the pop-popping of the fireworks. But before they could react, the man's face retreated beneath the dragon's tail and it moved on down the street.

"Oh, my gosh!" Grant exclaimed, letting out the breath he had been holding. "We've got to find Christina and Ellie!"

The girls were clapping and dancing to the loud drums as Grant and Ethan raced up to them. The boys were pale and sweaty, and Grant seemed very upset. Christina grabbed his shoulders. "What's wrong?"

Grant was on the verge of tears, so he turned away and shrugged his shoulders. He didn't want to admit that the man had frightened him so badly. He took a deep breath to pull himself together. "The security guard from the coin shop just popped out from under that big dragon!" he shouted, pointing down the street.

Christina looked up to see the dragon turn a corner. "It'll be OK, Grant!" She patted him on his back and looked down the street. "From now on, we all stick together," she stated firmly.

A few minutes later, Papa waved to the kids and announced it was time to return to the hotel.

18

CHOCOLATE EVIDENCE

Back at the hotel, the boys had gone to their room and the girls relaxed at the dining room table. Christina, deep in thought about the events of the day, absently snapped the lock on the metal box up and down.

Mimi entered, wearing the bright red kimono she had purchased in Chinatown. "Papa is downstairs getting a haircut," she said, "so I'm going to take a cat nap before the Mayor's Reception tonight at the Space Needle." She dabbed a few dots of face cream on her cheeks from a small jar she was holding. "You can never get too much beauty sleep, you know."

Christina's hand came to rest on the box. "Hey Mimi, can we look at the stuff in the box?" she asked.

"Why, I almost forgot it was here," she remarked. "We haven't had very much free time since we arrived, have we?" She headed toward the bedroom, wiggling her fingers in the air. "Yes, go ahead, but make sure you put everything back. We wouldn't want anything to get scratched."

You don't know the half of it, Christina thought. She hoisted the box under her arm, and hurried down the hall to Grant's room with Ellie. She tried the door, but it was locked. She knocked.

"What's the password?" Grant's muffled voice said.

"The password is 'open this door'," Christina answered, rattling the doorknob.

"Sorry, no girls allowed," Grant stated.

Christina heard the boys giggling behind the door. "OK, I guess Ellie and I will just have to study the contents of the metal box by ourselves!" She grinned at Ellie, and silently mouthed, "Three, two, one."

Grant threw open the door. "Why didn't you say so in the first place?" he said.

"Boys," Christina said, rolling her eyes. She set the box down on his bed and opened the lid. She carefully lifted the mold used to make the tokens and examined it. It was made of metal, and was spring-loaded on one end to open and close. It had round, metal engravings on the other end to make the tokens.

"Hey, it sort of looks like the salad tongs Mimi uses to get lettuce out of a bowl," Grant observed.

Christina set the mold down, opened her backpack, and took out the two tokens they had carried around all day. She returned the real token to the box and rubbed her fingers over the surface of the one Mr. Tom said was a silver dollar. He had been right when he said the surface felt rubbery. She set it down on the bed for the others to examine.

"So," she said, "we know this silver dollar was covered with something to make it look like a token." She bit her bottom lip in thought. "But why? Were they testing the mold to see if they could make silver dollars?"

Grant picked up the clunky token mold and examined it. He started rummaging through his backpack and pulled out two chocolate bars.

Christina could see where this was going and tried to reason with him. "You are not planning to do what I think you're planning to do, are you?"

Grant grabbed the mold and chocolate bars and moved to the desk.

She followed closely behind him. "Do you want to be grounded for the rest of your life?" Christina asked, trying to snatch the mold from her brother.

Grant set the mold down and lifted one of the silver dollars out of the box. He wiggled the candy bars. "Good, they're soft, so that should work for what I need to do." After taking off the wrappers, he put one candy bar on one engraving plate, and the other candy bar on the other one. He started to squeeze the two halves together. "This is how the coating was probably pushed down onto the silver dollars," he remarked.

Christina leaned over the desk, as Grant carefully positioned the silver dollar between the chocolate bars. As he pressed down on the two halves of the mold, the soft chocolate oozed through the sides. Grant wiped his finger around the rim to get rid of the excess chocolate. He sucked the chocolate off his finger and licked his hand.

"OK, that's gross!" Christina exclaimed.

Grant ignored her and went back to work. When he opened the press, the same imprint as the real token was visible, and the Coliseum had the extra line in the roof. Using his forefinger, he slowly traced the indentations on the chocolate. "I knew it!" Grant shouted. "And I bet this is the very mold they used to do it, too!"

Christina tapped her finger to her lips. "So they weren't trying to make silver dollars, they were coating the silver dollars to make them look like tokens!" she said. She looked up at Ellie and Ethan. "To steal them!"

"Yeah," Grant said, "and this would make it easier to get them out of the building!"

Christina started pacing. "But when we were researching on the Internet, there was no talk about a silver dollar robbery at the World's Fair," she remarked. She paused in front of the box. Mindlessly, her fingers wandered over the other items and stopped on the picture. She absently picked it up and casually looked at it. Suddenly she shouted, "Oh my gosh! Oh my gosh!"

"What is it, Christina?" asked Grant.

Christina turned the picture toward the kids. "It's the same picture we saw on display at KeyArena," she said. "The men were much younger then, but there was no mistaking them in the picture. Only now we know that it's the security guard from the Ferris wheel, and Hawk Eyes from the coin shop!" Christina shuddered.

Papa suddenly entered the room to tell the kids it was time to get ready to go to the Mayor's Reception. "What's going on?" he asked. "It smells like a chocolate factory in here!"

Grant smiled. "Hi Papa!" he said. He didn't know it, but chocolate stuck to his teeth, smeared his lips, and caked in his hair, making it stick out in coarse tufts. Christina whisked the mold behind her back.

Papa peered at Grant over the black reading glasses perched on his nose. "You've been digging into dessert before we've even had dinner, haven't you?"

Grant giggled. "Well, I..." he began.

Papa took Grant by the hand and headed for the door. "To the showers with you, little man!"

DING! DING! Ellie's phone lit up with a text from her grandmother. "Grandma is here to pick us up to get ready for the Mayor's Reception," she said. "See you tonight," she called, and quickly left the room with Ethan.

Now that Christina was alone with the picture in her hand, she noticed a few more things about the surroundings and the men in the picture. She now knew how the two guards had direct contact with the silver dollars. But who was the third man in the picture?

19

SHOP UNTIL YOU DROP

The group piled into the hotel van and headed out. The Space Needle drifted into Christina's view as she stared out the window. Its silhouette glowed against the Seattle skyline amidst the blues and pinks of twilight. "Gosh," Christina said, "it looks magical!"

As the family walked through the glass doors of the Space Needle Pavilion, people chatted while they waited for the mayor to arrive. Waiters in black tuxedos served beverages in crystal glasses. Mimi wore a red silk pantsuit with a sparkly rhinestone collar. Papa wore a navy blue suit, his black cowboy hat, and black boots.

Mimi handed Grant a small plate with an array of mini appetizers to sample. When he saw Ethan, he waved him over and complained. "Dressing up twice in the same week is so totally not fair," he said.

Grant showed Christina and Ellie his saucer-sized plate. "Mimi says this is finger food, but I don't know what that means," he whispered.

"It means you eat it with your fingers, silly," Christina explained.

"Really?" Grant said with glee. He stuffed a mini hotdog into his mouth. "This is really great!" he mumbled through his mouthful of food. "I think I'll go get more food to eat with my fingers. Come on, Ethan." As the boys filled their plates, Grant glanced over a railing overlooking a huge store. "Oh, wow," he said. "What is that place?"

"It's the Space Base souvenir shop," Ethan replied. "It's a huge tourist attraction here at the Space Needle. And hey, it's still open!" They looked at one another, hurriedly set their food down on one of the tables, and ran to get the girls.

Grant tugged on Papa's arm. "Papa, can we go to the souvenir shop downstairs for a few minutes, please?" He gestured to the railing.

Papa looked at his watch and glanced over at Mimi. Without stopping her conversation with the mayor, or looking up, she gave a quick nod.

"How does she do that?" Christina wanted to know. Gesturing to the stairs, she said to the others, "Come on, let's go have a look-see."

As he entered the store, Grant grinned with delight at the many treasures before him. "Wow, just look at this place," he said. He didn't know which direction to go first.

He took a step forward, but Christina put out her hand to stop him. She had an eerie feeling that she was being watched. She glanced around and up. "Look!" she said, pointing. Grant followed her finger with his eyes. There, just above them, the security guard with the white mustache seemed to be searching for something—or someone. Suddenly, he looked down, and their eyes met. He shook his fist and pushed away from the railing. He was coming after them!

Christina quickly motioned to Ethan and Ellie. "Quick, let's huddle!" she ordered. When they all came together, she said, "That creepy security guard from the Ferris wheel is here. He saw us and he's coming!" She looked into their worried faces. "I have a plan, but we must be very quiet and stick together." She wanted to reassure them, so she put out her hand. Grant rested his hand on Christina's hand, Ellie put her hand over Grant's hand, and Ethan piled his over Ellie's hand.

Christina raised her eyes, scanning the door. "OK, ready?" she asked.

"Ready!" they whispered, and followed Christina.

The angry guard entered the shop. "I saw you kids down here," he barked. "You might as well give up!"

The shop was a round shape, so Christina knew that no matter which way they went, they would end up where they started. She crouched low, and the kids did too. They crept quietly in the opposite direction of the guard's voice. After a few minutes, Christina stopped by some shelves to listen.

Grant noticed a display of plastic snow globes sitting next to him. He picked one up and shook it, making it snow over a miniature Space Needle. "Cool!" he whispered, as he set it back down on the shelf.

Christina frowned at him. "Will you stop shopping and get serious?" she scolded. She looked at Ellie. "I don't like it," Christina remarked. "He's being too quiet."

"Ah-ha!" The security guard leaped out from behind a rack of T-shirts.

Startled, the kids shrieked. "Ahhhhhhhhh!"

The man loomed over them and said, "I've got you now!"

"Hey, you kids!" Papa's booming voice flowed down from the railing above the shop. The man looked up and quickly ran away. When Papa's smiling face appeared over the railing, the kids sighed in relief. "Come on!" he said, "it's time to head up to the observation deck."

The man in the light gray fedora with the small red feather had been watching, and headed upstairs too, in a hidden service elevator.

20

SPACE CAGE

"Hello, everyone," Connie said, greeting the crowd at the Mayor's Reception. "His Honor has arrived, so it's time to move to the observation deck." The doors to the elevator opened, and the visitors waited their turn to board the elevators.

The kids boarded the elevator with Mimi, Papa, and five or six other people. Just as the doors were about to close, a man's arm shot through to keep the door from closing. Christina looked up and tried not to scream. Hawk Eyes had gotten on the elevator! The kids quickly slid behind the adults so he couldn't see them.

When the doors opened, Hawk Eyes left, but the kids still moved among the safety of the adults.

A breeze whipped through the chilly night air as they stepped out onto the observation deck. As the adults moved on, Christina stopped the kids. "I think something is going to go down here tonight," she predicted. "Both security guards are here, and I feel sure that's not a coincidence." She glanced left and spied the security guard with the white mustache. He saw them too, and started heading their way.

"Now I'm 100 percent sure it's not a coincidence," Christina said. "Split up and RUN!" The kids scattered in different directions.

Christina and Grant ran toward the elevator. Suddenly, the doors opened and Jenna waved them in. "Hurry!" she said.

"Jenna!" Christina exclaimed, panting, as the doors closed. "Are we glad to see you!" She was so happy to see her that she didn't realize Jenna hadn't pushed the Down button.

"Hey, what gives?" Grant said, noticing that the elevator wasn't moving.

Christina looked into Jenna's eyes and knew she had betrayed them. "Why are you doing this?" she asked.

Jenna blinked back tears. "Because he's my grandpa, and I love him," she said, and pushed the button to re-open the doors.

As the doors opened, the security guard with the white mustache tried to step inside. Christina and Grant pushed past him and ran back toward the Mayor's Reception.

The kids ran-walked through the back of the reception area. Mimi was speaking with the mayor and waved to them as they went past. They ran back inside and up a short flight of steps, where they found themselves in a roped-off area. When Christina looked to her right, she saw a room with the door propped open with a light on. The sign on the door said, "Space Cage, No Admittance."

She scrambled to the door. "This name was in the journal, Grant," she said excitedly.

"This is where the silver dollars are!" She grabbed the handle to go inside.

Grant backed away. "I don't think we should go in there," he said softly. His voice quivered.

"Then wait here," Christina whispered, and charged inside. Cartons were stacked from floor to ceiling, but fresh scrape marks in the dust on the floor suggested that someone had recently moved some of them.

She followed the marks and saw five cartons stacked in a corner. They were marked with a sticker that read, "1962 World's Fair Tokens." Christina looked closer and saw a drawing of the Coliseum with an extra line on the roof. "Oh, my gosh!" she exclaimed. "Grant, look!" She turned to tell him to come inside when she noticed a scrap of paper on the floor. She picked it up and opened it.

THEY KNOW
YOU'RE IN HERE!
HIDE!

Christina's head snapped up. Hide? Hide where? Practically every inch of the room was filled with boxes. Just as she turned to flee, both security guards blocked the door. "Well, look who we found!" Hawk Eyes snarled.

Christina knew they wanted the coins. She stepped in front of the cartons and hoped they didn't see her legs trembling.

The men took a step closer. "Get out of our way, missy," the security guard with the white mustache said. "We've been waiting more than 50 years to get our hands on that money!"

"And you'll wait another hundred years before you get it!" a voice shouted. The guards turned, and there stood the man in the light gray fedora with the small red feather.

Before anyone could react, they heard running footsteps and a booming voice yell, "STOP!" Papa's head had barely cleared the doorway when he shouted, "Don't any of you even think about taking a step toward my granddaughter!"

21

HIDDEN IN PLAIN SIGHT

"Papa!" Christina screeched, as the imposing figure of her grandfather entered the room. Two policemen followed closely behind him. Both guards put their hands up and backed away slowly. Christina ran to Papa. He hugged her briefly and guided her into Mimi's outstretched arms. Connie, Grant, Ethan, and Ellie stood next to Mimi.

"Christina, don't be mad at me for leaving," Grant said. "When I heard those men, I went to get Papa." He peered at the man wearing the fedora and said, "Hey, I've seen you before!" He searched his memory. "I remember now!" Grant continued. "It's your hat. You're the man I bumped into on the airplane. But who are you?"

"I'm Old Mike," he said, tipping his hat.

"Well, Old Mike," Papa said, folding his arms across his chest. "Suppose you start explaining."

Old Mike nodded. "Back in 1962," he began, "when the silver dollars arrived at the World's Fair, the three of us were hired as security guards. We were fresh out of high school. I didn't know it, but those two had already planned to intercept the silver dollar promotion before it got to the mailroom." He motioned to the five cartons on the floor. "Then they filled these cartons with the coated silver dollars, so they could sneak them out a little at a time."

Christina stepped forward. "Why didn't you go to the police?" she asked.

"I was afraid of those two guys," Old Mike admitted, and hung his head. "They didn't know I saw them coat the coins, then use the mold to make them resemble the other tokens. I knew I couldn't stop what they'd already done, but I could stop them from doing any more. And I could stop them from getting the silver dollars out of the Space Needle."

He looked at Grant and Christina. "So, after they left for the night," Old Mike explained, "I packed up their mold, the tokens, silver dollars, my journal with the money coordinates, and the picture of the three of us in the box. I locked it and stashed it in a hidden storeroom where it would stay hidden forever. But it resurfaced during the Space Needle renovations. I tried to purchase it at the auction, but your grandmother beat me to it."

"So where are the silver dollars?" a police officer asked.

Old Mike smiled. "I hid them in plain sight." He pointed to the sealed cartons marked "1962 World's Fair Tokens."

Everyone turned when a tall man stepped into the room. "Hello, everyone," he said. "I'm Detective Bill, Old Mike's grandson."

"And just where do you fit into all this?" Papa demanded.

Christina looked up at the man. "The phone call," she said. "It was you Old Mike called the night of the auction," she said.

"And the person who has been following us," Grant chimed in.

"And the man leaving us the warning clues," Christina added. "But why?"

"Christina, the men who did this were still at large," Detective Bill explained. "Once they found out you had the silver dollar token, and other evidence against them, they would have stopped at nothing to get them— no matter what."

The two policemen grabbed the arms of the security guards and led them toward the door. One of the police officers motioned to the cartons. "We'll need to take this evidence to the station." He tried to lift one of the cartons and grunted. "I think we're going to need to get an electric cart up here," he said.

Christina smiled. *The silver dollars are safe now,* she thought.

22

A GOLD KEY AND SILVER DOLLARS

Christina and Grant waited to go onstage in the Space Needle banquet room. They heard the mayor say, "And now, may I present Christina and Grant." Everyone in the room applauded loudly, and the kids stepped onto the stage. Ethan and Ellie soon joined them, helping the mayor carry a huge golden key made of cardboard.

"I'm happy to report," the mayor announced, "that the thousands of silver dollars recovered from the 1962 World's Fair robbery weighed 295 pounds, and their value today is more than $60,000. That money has been generously donated to further the renovations to the Space Needle."

He turned to face Christina and Grant. "To Christina and Grant," he said, "whose intelligence and bravery helped bring these criminals to justice, we give you our thanks, and the key to our city."

Mimi and Papa were sitting at a table with Connie, Detective Bill, and Old Mike. They all jumped to their feet and applauded. Papa put two fingers to his mouth and whistled.

Once the ceremony ended, Christina and Grant hurried to their grandparents' table. "Look," Grant said, "the mayor gave us each a silver dollar from the 1962 World's Fair!"

"Wow!" Papa said. "That's very special! What are you going to do with it?"

"I'm going to have it covered in chocolate!" Grant declared.

"What?" Papa asked.

"Don't ask," Christina said with a giggle.

Papa took Mimi's hand. "I'm sorry you didn't get to read the journal to get some mystery ideas before you gave it back to Old Mike," he said.

Christina hugged her grandmother tightly. "Don't you worry about that, Mimi," she said. "Have we got a story for you!"

The End

Now...go to:

www.carolemarshmysteryclub.com

so you can:

- Read excerpts from other books!

- Enjoy Book Club activities!

- Go on a Scavenger Hunt!

- Take a Pop Quiz!

- Enter a contest to win a free mystery!

- Join the Fan Club...and MUCH MORE!

GLOSSARY

analyze: to study or examine something carefully

auction: a public sale where things are sold to those who offer to pay the most for them

fedora: a felt hat with a wide brim and indented crown

fundraiser: a social function or activity used to raise money for a particular purpose

pavilion: a building that usually has open sides and is used for parties, concerts, or other events

pungent: having a sharply strong taste or smell

reverently: done in a very respectful way

savory: having a pleasant taste or smell

speculate: to think about something and make guesses about it

SAT GLOSSARY

disheveled: untidy or messy

mimic: (*verb*) to imitate someone's actions or words

oblong: having an elongated shape, as a rectangle or an oval

offhand: without previous thought or preparation

undermine: damage or weaken someone or something

Enjoy this exciting excerpt from:

THE MYSTERY AT Yellowstone National Park

1

BELIEVE IT OR NOT!

Grant began to stir in his rumpled hotel bed sheets, rolling from side to side as he did every morning as he woke up. This morning he had the strange sensation that someone was watching him. He cracked open one eye to see a small lens right in front of his face.

"Christina! What are you doing?" Grant croaked. His sister was standing directly over him with her brand new video camera pointing down at him. Grant whipped the sheet over his head and buried down deep into his feather bed.

"Gooood morning, little brother! It's a marvelous day for a snowmobile ride!" Christina turned her camera toward the window and began filming the snow-covered rolling hills of Cody, Wyoming. "Wow! I can't believe that some people get to look at this view every day. It sure is different than little ol' Peachtree City, Georgia."

Grant slowly crawled out of the covers and sat upright. He rubbed his fingers over his face and through his tousled blond hair. "The only scenery I want to see right now is a loaded breakfast buffet," he said. "I hope they serve real sourdough pancakes out here in the West!"

Christina and Grant had arrived in Cody the night before, along with their grandparents, Mimi and Papa. The kids often traveled with their grandparents while Mimi did research for the children's mystery books she wrote. Mimi always said that the ability to give her grandchildren excitement AND an education was the best job in the world!

Wyoming was one of Papa's favorite parts of the country. One of his fondest memories was a snowmobile tour of Yellowstone National Park that he and Mimi had taken years earlier. A cowboy through and through, Papa was excited to recreate that expedition for his grandchildren. The stop in Cody was a brief layover on the way to what Papa described as a "journey through one of the United States' most valuable treasures." He couldn't wait to put on his cowboy hat and boots and share that treasure with Grant and Christina.

There was a knock at the door adjoining the kids' room to their grandparents' suite.

"Kiddos! You up?" Papa hollered. "We've gotta get a move on—mud pots and geysers and bison await!"

"We're up, Papa!" replied Christina. "We're getting our snow bibs on and packing up our stuff." Christina and Grant loved to snow ski every year with their parents, so luckily they had all the cold weather clothing they would need on this tour. Snowmobiling through the park would be all kinds of fun—but since Yellowstone gets an average of 150 inches of snow every year, it would also be all kinds of cold!

Christina stowed her video camera in her backpack. The kids quickly got dressed, gathered their things, and headed to meet Mimi and Papa for breakfast. They were looking forward to filling up with food, and also filling up with the details Papa and Mimi would give them about their trip.

"Papa, when are we getting our snowmobiles?" Grant asked. "I've been practicing my driving skills on my video game. I'm ready to speed all around the trails!" He plopped down at the restaurant table with Frisbee-sized pancakes and greasy bacon spilling off his plate.

Christina's eyes got huge as she put granola and fruit into her yogurt. She had heard there were dangers to look out for throughout the national park, but she never thought it would be her brother on a snowmobile! Luckily, Papa quickly put her mind at ease.

"Oh, I don't think so, cowboy!" Papa said. "You must have a driver's license to operate a snowmobile. The last time I checked, you didn't have one. So you will be RIDING—not driving on this trip."

As Papa piloted the *Mystery Girl* to Cody the night before, Christina sat in the back of the plane finishing up a fantastic book she'd begun reading that very morning, so she hadn't yet asked her grandmother what this winter excursion was all about.

"Ok, Mimi," Christina began, "what's so great about Yellowstone? Why do you and Papa love it so much?"

"Yeah, Mimi," said Grant, "we've been to a national park before. Why is this one any different?"

Mimi pulled her sparkly glasses from her face and smiled at her grandson. "Grant, Yellowstone isn't just *A* national park. It is *THE* national park—the very first national park in the entire world."

"All thanks to President Ulysses S. Grant," said Papa. "He realized that the land and the water and the wildlife here were valuable to the world. So in 1872, he declared that the area would be a national park. As it says on the Roosevelt Arch up at the North Entrance of the park, 'Yellowstone is for the benefit and enjoyment of the people.'"

"So what are we going to see?" asked Christina, popping a last grape into her mouth.

"Oh, Christina," said Mimi, "the park is full of sights and sounds and smells that you could never imagine!"

"That's right," said Papa. "As a matter of fact, when the 19th century explorers began telling the stories about what they saw in this wilderness, people didn't believe them."

"What couldn't they believe?" asked Grant skeptically.

"They couldn't believe what you are getting ready to see on this trip," said Mimi. "Yellowstone National Park is a boiling, bubbling, steaming, gushing, spewing, sizzling, smelly place!"

Grant looked out the window at the sun coming up and glistening off the powder-white snow. "It's freezing cold and there is a ton of snow outside," he said. "I don't see how anything can boil and steam in the dead of winter."

"That's what's so amazing about Yellowstone, young 'un," said Papa. "And wait until you see the wildlife—oh, the animals we'll see! Bison, bears, deer, wolves, elk, coyotes, eagles..." his voice trailed off.

Mimi loved to see Papa's eyes light up

and the permanent grin attach to his face when he was out in this part of the country.

Christina grabbed her video camera out of her backpack and hit the 'Record' button. "Land that is boiling and steaming? This I gotta see! And film, of course!" she said. "So when do we start?"

"If Grant will wipe that syrup off his chin, we can start right now!" said Papa. "We'll commandeer some snowmobiles and be on our way!"

Grant was excited but also a bit skeptical. As he zipped up his heavy coat and headed to the door with his sister and his grandparents, he secretly hoped that something interesting would crop up during their trip that would add a little thrill to their journey!

He wouldn't have to wait long.

2

REPETITIVE ROUTES

Molly Jane Edwards put rubber bands around her hair braids, stuck her glasses on her face, and let out a sigh. Every year Molly Jane and her parents made the same trip from their house in Jackson Hole, Wyoming to Yellowstone National Park. Her parents were obsessed with the place! For hours, they would watch the mud pots bubble and belch. Or they'd examine and analyze the churning, swirling hot springs and thermal pools or spewing geysers. Her dad could explain how algae could change the color of the water as it tumbled over the Lower Falls, the highest waterfall in the park. Her mom loved the wildflowers and the trees in spring and would **continuously** chirp out their names in English and in Latin!

Without even realizing it, Molly Jane had become something of an expert of the science behind the sights and sounds of Yellowstone. Her parents were great teachers and it was hard not to get swept up in their excitement about these natural wonders, even as they were headed to Flagg Ranch at the park's South Entrance for the sixth time in as many years.

At least this time would be a little different since they were going in the middle of winter. Molly was excited that they would be traveling by snow coach instead of by car. Hopefully there wouldn't be as many traffic jams with snowmobiles and snow coaches as there were with cars during the height of tourist season. Maybe the snow and the trails would shed new light on some of these places in Yellowstone that she knew so well.

If only I had a friend to go with me this time, thought Molly Jane. If only there was a new way to look at the park or a more interesting way to experience its sights. Little did she know there were other kids headed to Yellowstone with the exact same idea!

3
SURPRISE SURPRISE!

Gunny Mitchell's great-great-grandfather was a world-class hiker back in his day. He had traveled through some of the most scenic and most dangerous areas in the entire United States, documenting his travels in his journals. His expeditions were revered among hikers to this very day.

"Remind me, Dad, if great-great-grandfather James was such a good hiker, then why did he die by falling into a hot spring at Yellowstone?" Gunny asked his father as they were packing up their camping gear.

"It was an unfortunate accident, Gunny," replied his father. "He stumbled into a spring while hiking at night. Back in those days, the hot springs at Yellowstone were not marked. If it was dark and someone could not see where they were walking, they could fall in and die a very gruesome death. The water in hot springs can be more than 200 degrees Fahrenheit."

Gunny shuddered. He had burned his fingers on a hot roll the night before—he couldn't imagine what 200 degrees would feel like!

Gunny and his dad were driving down to the North Entrance of Yellowstone from Bozeman, Montana. Mr. Mitchell was an animal researcher, specializing in wildlife of the West—bison, elk, moose, and bears especially. Because of his dad, Gunny loved the outdoors and the animals that lived there.

Gunny was big and strong for his age, the perfect size for a middle school kid who helped his father on wildlife research trips. Mr. Mitchell was documenting winter habitats of endangered wildlife in Yellowstone and offered to take Gunny along with him. When they reached the North Entrance, he surprised Gunny with the fact that they would be taking snowmobiles through the park to have a little fun while they were working.

Mr. Mitchell would have been surprised himself if he had known what Gunny had planned. In the attic of their house, the boy had found a faded Yellowstone trail map scribbled with notes, lines, and markings that obviously belonged to his great-great-grandfather James. There was a note attached to the front that read:

> If you have this map, then I am no longer hiking this earth.
> To you, I leave clues to something more valuable than gold;
> More precious than gems; a treasure of a lifetime.
> Its owner will only profit from its riches!

Gunny had the map and the note hidden in his backpack (his father jokingly referred to it as his "Gunny Sack"). He didn't want to tell his dad that he had other ideas about their trip through Yellowstone because he knew his father's research was important. But maybe, just maybe, he could do a little treasure hunting while they were there. He wished he was an expert at following clues because the first clue already had him stumped. Maybe he would run into tourists or park rangers who could help him, he thought.